the Pagemaster

D0406457

CLASSIC SERIES

TREASURE ISLAND

Adapted from the novel by Robert Louis Stevenson

the Pagemaster™

CLASSIC SERIES

TREASURE ISLAND

Adapted by **Margaret Webb**   Illustrated by **Tom Taylor**

the Pagemaster™ Classic Series was inspired by *the* Pagemaster™, a feature film presented by Twentieth Century Fox in association with Turner Pictures. TM & © 1994 Twentieth Century Fox Film Corporation and Turner Pictures, Inc. All rights reserved. *Treasure Island* adaptation: Text copyright and illustration copyright © 1994 Tribute Publishing Inc. Published in Canada by Tribute Publishing Inc., Don Mills, Ontario. Printed in Canada by Quebecor.   ISBN 1-896298-06-0

the Pagemaster™

presents

TREASURE ISLAND

Adapted from the novel by Robert Louis Stevenson

My name is Jim Hawkins.

I was asked to write the story of a voyage to Treasure Island. I hold nothing back except the exact directions of that island, because there is still treasure hidden there.

But I will start, first, with the arrival of an old seaman who came plodding to the Admiral Benbow Inn, owned by my father. I remember him as if it were yesterday. He was a tall, strong, heavy man; his hair was tied in a pigtail that fell over the shoulders of his soiled blue coat; he had a scar from a sabre cut across one cheek. He squinted and looked out to sea before breaking out into singing that old sea song:

*"Fifteen men on the
dead man's chest,
Yo-ho-ho, and a
bottle of rum!"*

He rapped on the door. He asked for a glass of rum and if our inn had much company. When my father said it was a lonely place, he said, "Well, then, this is the place for me."

His name was Bill Bones, but he said we could call him captain. All day he hung around the cove with a brass telescope. He watched the sea and road for the approach of strangers. At night, he sat by the fire and sang wicked, wild sea-songs. He forced all the trembling guests at the inn to listen to his stories.

However, the captain grew quiet as a mouse when another seaman stayed at the Admiral Benbow.

The captain took me aside one day and promised me a silver fourpenny on the first of every month. All I had to do to earn it was keep my "weather-eye" open for a seafaring man with one leg.

The captain stayed on at our inn for months and months, and soon stopped paying for his room and board. My father did not have the heart to ask the captain to leave. I'm sure the bother of keeping the captain happy led to my father's early death. He died not long after the captain's arrival at our inn.

We did not have long to mourn his death.

One January morning — a pinching, frosty morning — a pale figure came to the inn.

He was missing two fingers on his left hand. He asked to speak to his mate, Bill Bones. He described the captain as having a very pleasant way with him.

The mysterious visitor hid in the parlour to give Bill a "surprise" when the captain returned from his walk. The stranger must have been frightened a bit too, for he loosened his cutlass in its sheath.

When the captain saw him, he quietly gasped, "Black Dog!" Next instant I saw Black Dog running away, with the captain hotly pursuing. At the door, the captain aimed at Black Dog with a tremendous cut of his sword, which found its mark in our big signboard, Admiral Benbow. You may see the notch on it to this day.

That blow was not the last of the battles. The captain said it was his old sea chest that Black Dog and other seamen were after. The captain then said he had been first mate on a ship sailed by a captain named Flint and that Flint gave him a black spot when he lay dying.

"But what is the black spot?" I asked.

"That's a summons, mate. A call to action. I'll tell you if they get that. But you keep your weather-eye open, Jim, and I'll share with you equals, upon my honour."

About three weeks passed when I saw someone else on the road. He was plainly blind. "Boy," he said, "take me to the captain." I heard a voice so cruel and cold that I obeyed him at once.

This visitor told me to call out, "here's a friend for you captain." But when the captain saw the blind man, his face went pale.

The blind man passed something from his hand to the captain's, which closed upon it instantly. With that done, the blind beggar left.

The captain looked at the thing in his hand and said, "Ten o'clock! We'll do them yet."

Then he sprang to his feet and fell face first to the floor. He was struck dead.

I lost no time telling my mother all that I knew. We saw at once that we were in a dangerous situation. But some of the captain's money — if he really had any — was certainly owing to us.

"We have to get the key off that," said my mother, pointing to the captain. He was stretched out in the parlour, on his back, dead,

his eyes open.

Close to his hand was a piece of paper, blackened on one side. I could not doubt that this was the black spot. I found a message written on the other side, "You have till 10:00 o'clock tonight."

This news was good, for it was only six. We had four hours before the captain's ruthless enemies would arrive at the inn.

"Now, Jim," said my mother. "The key."

I tore open the captain's shirt at the neck. Sure enough, hanging on a bit of string, we found the key. We hurried upstairs to his sea chest.

We found nothing of any great value inside. There was some silver and trinkets. But under an old boat-cloak lay a sealed packet tied up in oilcloth.

Suddenly, I heard the tap-tapping of a blind man's stick outside the inn. But the door was latched and the tapping slowly died away.

"Mother," said I, "take the whole and let's be going."

I knew it was too dangerous to

stay at the inn alone. We decided to set out for help. We had not started out too soon. We were just at the little bridge, running towards the next village, when we heard footsteps. Our enemies began to arrive, seven or eight of them.

"Down with the door!" one cried.

"Bill's dead!" cried another.

"Search him and get the chest!"

"Bill's been searched already and nothin's left."

"It's these people of the inn — it's that boy," I heard the blind beggar say. "Scatter, lads, and find 'em."

Just then, the noise of horses greeted my ears. Four or five riders came in the moonlight. The blind beggar made a dash — right under the nearest of the horses. I hailed the horses. One was a lad from Dr. Livesey's; the rest were revenue officers.

I went back to the Admiral Benbow Inn. You cannot imagine a house in such a state of smash. The villains had broken everything in their search. I could see at once that my mother and I were ruined.

"What in fortune were they after?" asked one of the officers.

"Not money, I think," I replied. "I believe I have the thing in my breast pocket. I should like to take it to Dr. Livesey to have it put in safe keeping."

"Very well," he said.

I got a ride with the supervisor, and we rode hard all the way to Dr. Livesey's door. A servant led us into a great library, where Dr. Livesey sat with Squire Trelawney by a bright fire.

I had never seen the squire so close. He was a tall man, over six feet high, and his eyebrows were very black, which gave him a look of some temper, not bad, but quick and high.

I told the story of Bill Bones, first mate to Captain Flint, to the two men. Then I handed Dr. Livesey the oilskin packet.

The doctor looked the small pouch over as though his fingers were itching to open it, but he put it in his pocket.

"You have heard of this Flint, I suppose?" Dr. Livesey asked the squire.

"Heard of him?" replied the squire. "He was the bloodthirstiest buccaneer that ever sailed!"

"Supposing I have here in my pocket some clue to where Flint buried his treasure," said the doctor. "Would that treasure amount to much?"

"It will amount to this," said the squire. "If you have the clue, I will fit out a ship. I will take you and Hawkins here along, and I'll have that treasure if I search a year."

"Very well," said the doctor. "If Jim is agreeable, we'll open the packet."

The packet contained two things: a book and a sealed paper. The book was Bones's account-book. It had crosses that stood for the names of the ships that Flint's buccaneers had plundered.

The sealed paper contained a map of an island. The map had every detail that would be needed to bring a ship to safe anchorage on its shores. It also had three crosses of red ink. Beside the last was written: "Bulk of treasure here."

"Livesey," said the squire, "we'll set sail in three weeks with the best ship, the choicest crew in England. Hawkins shall come as cabin boy, you as ship's doctor, and I as admiral."

THE SEA COOK

It took longer than the squire imagined before we were ready for

9

sea. But finally a letter arrived from Bristol for Dr. Livesey. The squire had found a ship, the *Hispaniola*, and a half dozen men. But a stroke of fortune took him to a public house run by an old sailor, Long John Silver. Silver, as his friends called him, had lost a leg.

Silver knew all the seafaring men in Bristol. Within a few days, the squire and Silver had put together a crew of the toughest old salts imaginable.

I got ready to sail. I said good-bye to my mother and the cove where I had lived since I was born, and to the dear old Admiral Benbow Inn. One of my last thoughts there was of the captain, who had so often strode along the beach.

When I met up with the squire in Bristol I cried, "When do we sail?"

"We sail tomorrow!" he said.

He then gave me a note addressed to John Silver. He told me where I could find Silver's little tavern along the docks. I set off.

Now, to tell you the truth, from the first mention of Long John in Squire Trelawney's letter, I was afraid he might be the very one-legged sailor whom the captain had asked me to watch out for.

But one look at the man before

me changed my mind. I had seen the captain, Black Dog, and the blind beggar, and I thought I knew what a buccaneer looked like. That was very different from this clean, pleasant-tempered man.

"Mr. Silver?" I asked, giving him the squire's letter.

He seemed to me to give something of a start. At that moment a man rose suddenly and ran for the door.

"Stop him," I cried. "It's Black Dog!"

"Who did you say he was?" asked Silver. "Well, I don't care who it is. He hasn't paid his bill. Run after him!"

Two of the other customers leapt up to catch the man. Silver spoke to me in a flattering way, but my suspicions about Silver were reawakened upon finding Black Dog at his tavern.

Silver was too clever, too ready for me. The men soon came back, breathless. They said they had lost Black Dog in the crowd. Silver said they must report this at once to the squire. I was ready then to believe everything Long John Silver said, for he seemed to be honest about this.

On our walk to the inn where the squire and Dr. Livesey were staying, I began to see that he was one of the best of possible shipmates. The squire and Dr. Livesey agreed.

The *Hispaniola* was anchored some way out in the harbour. We rowed a small boat out to her. When we went aboard, we met the captain. He was a sharp-looking man, who seemed angry with everything on board. Captain Smollett spoke plain to the squire.

"Sir," said the captain, "I don't like this cruise; I don't like the men; and I don't like my officer. That's short and sweet."

"Perhaps, sir, you don't like the ship," said the squire, angrily.

"She seems a clever craft," said the captain, "though I haven't tried her."

Dr. Livesey cut in. "Tell us why you don't like the cruise."

"I was hired, sir, on what we call sealed orders," said the captain. "But I find that all the sailors know more than I do. I don't call that fair, do you?"

"No," said Dr. Livesey, "I don't."

"I learn we are after treasure," replied the captain. "I don't like treasure voyages, especially when they are secret. But the secret has even been told to the parrot."

"Silver's parrot?" asked the squire.

"It's a way of saying someone's blabbed. And I believe neither of you gentlemen know what this is all about. But I'll tell you, it's life or death."

"That's all," said Dr. Livesey. "We take the risk. Now, tell us captain, what you want."

"I want the gunpowder and guns moved from the front of the ship to under the cabin. I want you and your company to take berths there. And this map of the island, with crosses to show where the treasure is ...."

"I never told that!" cried the squire.

"Well keep it secret even from me," the captain warned.

"I see," said the doctor. "You wish us to guard the stern of the ship and keep this treasure hunt a secret. Otherwise, you fear a mutiny."

"I ask you to take certain precautions," said the captain. "Or let me resign. That's all. You'll find I'll do my duty."

"Squire," said the doctor. "I believe you have hired two honest men — Captain Smollett and John Silver."

We worked through the night and at first light the *Hispaniola* began her voyage to Treasure Island.

Three things happened before we arrived at the island, which I must tell you.

The first was that the officer, Mr. Arrow, turned out worse than the captain feared. He did not have the respect of the men and drank shamelessly. Nobody was much surprised when one dark night he went missing.

"Overboard!" said the captain. "Well, that saves us from putting him in irons."

The second thing is about John Silver. Silver worked as the ship's cook — the men called him Barbecue. All the crew respected and even obeyed him. He had a way of speaking to each man in a special way. He was always kind.

Some who had sailed with Silver before were sad to see that he could only work as a cook because of his missing leg.

"Come away, Hawkins," Silver would say to me when I wandered by his galley, the ship's kitchen. "Come and have a yarn with John. Nobody more welcome in

my galley than yourself, my son."

He told me stories about his parrot, Cap'n Flint.

"That bird," Silver said, "may be 200 years old and if anybody's seen more wickedness, it must be the devil himself. I calls her Cap'n Flint, after the famous buccaneer."

Before I describe the third incident, I must tell you that we made good time on the voyage. We were about one day off Treasure Island, and everyone was in the bravest of spirits.

It was just before sundown and all my work was done. The men were on deck watching for land. I wanted an apple so I went below, to the galley, to get one. But there was scarcely one apple left.

I had to crawl all the way into the apple barrel. I must have fallen asleep there, for I awoke with a start to a man's voice. It was Silver's. He was sitting not far off. Before I heard a dozen words, I understood that the lives of all the honest men aboard the ship depended on me.

Silver was flattering another

young man in the same way he had me. "I'll talk to you like a man," said Silver. "Here it is about gentlemen of fortune."

I began to understand that John Silver was planning to lead a mutiny and make himself captain of the ship.

"I'll finish with 'em at the island as soon as the treasure's on board," Silver told the sailor.

You may fancy the terror I was in, especially when Silver decided he wanted an apple. He was about to reach an arm into the barrel when someone shouted: "LAND HO!"

All the men ran up to the deck, allowing me to escape. In a moment, I followed them.

The moon was up and showed two hills in the distance. Between them a third, higher hill. I stood there watching the approach of land, but it was as if I was in a dream.

John Silver came closer to me. He did not know that I had overheard him from the apple barrel. Yet I was so horrified by his cruelty and power, that I shook when he laid his hand upon my arm.

"Ah," said he, "this here is a sweet spot, this island."

And clapping me in the friendliest way, he hobbled off and went below, I'm sure, to plan his takeover of the ship.

Captain Smollett and Dr. Livesey were talking together on deck. I was anxious to tell them my story. I came up with some excuse to get them alone below.

"Now, Hawkins," said the squire. "Speak up."

We were alone in the captain's cabin. I told them of Silver's conversation. When I was done, the captain said we must continue on as planned or the crew would sense something was wrong.

The captain counted how many men were loyal to our side: only seven out of twenty-six on board. Then the doctor spoke to me.

"Jim here," he said, "can help us more than anyone. The men are not shy with him, and Jim is a noticing lad."

"Jim," said the squire, "I put our faith in you."

MY SHORE ADVENTURE

That first morning the sun rose over the island, the men began to grumble. I thought this was a bad sign. Not a breath of air was moving. Mutiny hung over us

was the first of many mad ideas that contributed to saving our lives. With six of Silver's men left on board, we could not take the ship. It occurred to me to go ashore. I slipped over the side and curled up in the sails of one boat that was rowing to shore.

As it came to shore, I caught a branch of a tree and swung myself out and ran and ran until I could run no more. Then I heard the low tones of a human voice. I crawled under the nearest tree for cover.

like a thundercloud.

Long John Silver was hard at work. He was more pleasant than ever, trying to conceal the discontent of the crew.

Captain Smollett decided to let the men go ashore, hoping that our party of honest men might take the ship. But when the shore group was made up, six of Silver's men stayed behind on the big ship. Only 13, including Silver, were to go ashore.

Then an idea came to me. It

It was Silver, and he was speaking to one of the honest crew. But the man would not listen to any of Silver's evil plans. This brave fellow turned his back on the cook and set off walking for the beach. With a cry, Silver was on top of him then and twice buried his knife into the man's body.

I could not believe that murder had been done. How could I go back in the boats with these fellows? It was all over, I thought. Good-bye to the *Hispaniola*, good-bye to the doctor, good-bye to the squire and the captain. I faced either death by the mutineers or death by starvation on the island.

I ran as fast as I could. My mad dash brought me to the foot of a little hill and a forest of tall pines. I also ran into a fresh alarm.

I saw a figure leap from behind a pine. My heart thumped. It seemed dark and shaggy, a creature of the woods: a bear or man or monkey. Yet I saw it was a man.

To my wonder, he threw himself on his knees and held out his hands to me. I stopped.

"Who are you?" I asked.

"Ben Gunn," he answered. "I'm poor Ben Gunn, and I haven't spoken with anyone in three years."

"Three years!" I cried. "Were you shipwrecked?"

"Nay, mate, marooned."

I knew this word stood for some horrible punishment, common among buccaneers. A man would be put on some distant island and left behind with a gun and a little gunpowder.

"And what do you call yourself, mate?" he asked.

"Jim," I told him.

He begged me to believe that he was a good man. "And I'm rich," he said.

I felt sure that the poor man had gone crazy. Then he asked, "That ain't Flint's ship, is it?"

He seemed afraid of the thought. I felt sure that I had found an ally. I told him the story of our voyage. When I finished, he said, "You can put your trust in Ben Gunn."

He began to tell me his story of how he came to be marooned on Treasure Island.

"I were in Flint's ship when he buried the treasure," said Gunn. "He along with six strong seamen. I was watching the ship when Flint came up to it in a little boat, all by himself. The six men were all dead. It was battle, murder, and sudden death — him against six. Billy Bones was the mate; Long John was the quartermaster. They asked him where the treasure was. Flint said, 'Ah, you can go ashore, if you like, and stay!'

"Well, I went back with Flint but soon came back to the island on another ship to look for the treasure we left behind. When we sighted this island, I said, 'Boys, here's Flint's treasure; let's find it.' Twelve days we looked for it. Every day the sailors cursed me more. Finally they said, 'Benjamin Gunn, here's a musket and a pickax. You stay here and find Flint's money for yourself.' Well, I've been here, the man of the island, for three years."

"How am I or you to get on board the ship?" I asked.

"There's my boat," he said. "I keep her under the white rock."

At that moment, a cannon fired. All the island awoke to the sound.

"They have begun to fight," I said. "Follow me!"

THE STOCKADE

A quarter mile in front of me, a Union Jack, the flag of Great Britain, flew in the air above a stockade, a log-house that was well protected by a fence. I called out to the log-house, for Gunn said the pirates would not be flying the Union Jack overhead.

I looked out to the *Hispaniola* and, sure enough, the Jolly Roger — the black flag of piracy — was flying from her peak.

As the doctor told me later, he and Hunter set out for shore in search of me. They took muskets and food. On returning, the pirates were drunk.

The doctor came up with a plan. They put Redruth by the cabin behind a mattress for pro-tection. The captain and the squire took up pistols. They called the leader of the pirates over to them. Then the captain called out to the other five pirates on board.

"If any of you make a move, this man's dead."

Having caught the pirates by surprise, my friends loaded their boat up again and made for shore. They found the log-house and decided it was a good place to take shelter.

I skirted the woods to the rear of the log-house and was soon welcomed by my mates. The party inside was at their wits' end as to what to do. Stores of food and water were low. We might be starved into surrender. Our best hope was to try to kill off the buccaneers when they came near.

In this we had two allies, rum and the climate. The first kept the pirates singing late into the night at the beach. As for the second, the doctor said that the pirates would be on their backs within a week, sick with malaria. They were camping in a marsh.

That first night in the stockade was peaceful. The next morning, however, I was awakened by a cry of "truce!" John Silver stood outside the stockade waving a white cloth.

"Keep indoors, men," the captain told us. "Ten to one this is a trick."

The captain told us to take up muskets and guard the stockade, then he spoke to Silver.

"These poor lads have chosen me cap'n after your desertion, sir," Silver told the captain.

"We want that treasure," said Silver. "You would just as soon have your lives, I reckon. You have a chart, haven't you? You give us the chart to get the treasure and stop shooting poor seamen, and we'll offer you a choice. Either come aboard with us, and we'll drop you safe ashore some place, or we'll send the first ship we see here to pick you up."

The captain replied, "Now hear me. If you come up one by one, unarmed, I'll put you in irons and take you back to a trial in England. Otherwise, I'll put a bullet in your back next time I see you."

Silver spat. "Them that die will be the lucky ones." And he disappeared an instant afterwards into the trees.

The captain directed us to our posts. He told me to load muskets. And at that moment came news of the attack: a round of shots that hit the log-house.

They came from the north, seven or eight or nine sailors. They scrambled over the fence. We fired; three men fell. The other four climbed up onto the log-house and were upon us. One appeared in the doorway and fell with his cutlass upon the doctor.

Now the pirates were inside and we were without cover.

"Fight 'em in the open!" cried the captain.

The fighting was fierce but victory, for the time, was ours.

MY SEA ADVENTURE

There was no return of the mutineers. It gave us a chance to look after our wounded and get dinner ready.

After supper, the doctor took his hat and pistols, put the chart in his pocket, and set off briskly through the trees.

"Is the doctor crazy?" asked one of our shipmates.

"I take it," I said, "that the doctor has an idea. If I'm right, he's going now to see Ben Gunn."

I was right, as it appeared later. The next thing I did was a foolish, bold act. I took up some pistols, filled my pockets with biscuits and slipped out when no one was watching.

Setting out to find the white rock where Ben Gunn's boat was hidden, I searched for the white rock and, sure enough, found the boat.

At that moment, I took another notion. This was to paddle out, in the cover of night, and cut the *Hispaniola* adrift. Without anchor, she would be blown to shore. After the morning of fighting, I believed the mutineers would have nothing else in their hearts but to lift anchor and sail to sea. This I wanted to stop.

Soon the ship loomed before me, blacker than darkness. I was alongside the line that attached her to her anchor. I cut it, one strand after another, till the vessel drifted free.

I was almost swept against the side of the *Hispaniola* as it began to turn, spinning slowly, end to end, across the current.

I expected at any moment to be swamped. My hands came across a light rope that was trailing over the side of the ship. Instantly I grasped it and pulled myself aboard a second before my boat was crushed by the *Hispaniola*.

There were two watchmen still on board: the sailor we called Red-cap was on his back, stiff as a spike; Israel Hands was propped against the side of the ship, his chin on his chest, his face white as a candle beneath his tan.

The ship kept bucking like a horse, the sails filling on one tack, then another. At every jump of the schooner, Red-cap slipped to and fro while Hands, too, slid farther onto the deck. I began to feel sure they had killed each other.

While I was looking and wondering, Hands turned partly around and moaned. That moan of pain went right to my heart. Then I remembered the talk of mutiny over the apple barrel.

There was no time to lose. I went below. The pirates had broken everything open in their search for our treasure map. I gathered up some cheese and biscuits for myself and went back on deck to eat.

"That man's dead," said Hands, pointing to Red-cap. "And what might you want?"

"I've come aboard to take the ship," I said. "You'll please call me captain until further notice."

Hands looked at me sourly. He suggested striking a deal. In return for tying up the wound in his leg, he would direct me to sail the ship safely into North Inlet. There we could beach her on Treasure Island.

In three minutes I had the *Hispaniola* sailing easily before the wind along the coast of Treasure Island. I tied up the tiller and went below and got a soft silk handkerchief my mother had given me. With this, I tied up the great bleeding stab wound Hands had received in his thigh. He sat up straighter, spoke louder and clearer.

Hands showed me how to sail from where he sat on the deck. Now that the ship was steady, he said it was time to throw Red-cap's body into sea. I refused.

"You can kill the body, Mr. Hands, but not the spirit," I replied.

I refused partly because I knew something else was working in Hands's mind. He asked me to fetch him some wine from below.

"All right," I answered.

He had a plan and I meant to find out what it was. I hurried down below, slipped off my shoes, and ran quietly to the front of the ship. There, I mounted a ladder and popped my head back up on deck. Hands had risen to his hands and knees and was reaching for a knife. He hid it in his jacket.

Hands was now armed and meant me to be his next victim. Yet I felt sure I could trust him on one point. We both wanted to land safely. And I believed I could out-dodge a wounded man, for playing dodge was a boy's game.

I fetched Hands his wine and got back to the business of landing the ship. The excitement of landing made me forget the knife Hands had hidden in his jacket. I might have fallen without a struggle, but something made me turn my head. Sure enough, Hands was coming at me, the knife in his hand.

We both cried out. Mine was a cry of terror, his of fury. He threw himself at me and I leapt sideways. As I did, I let go of the tiller, which struck Hands across the chest and stopped him for the moment.

I drew my pistol from my pocket, took cool aim, and pulled the trigger. The hammer fell, but there was no flash or sound. It was ruined with sea water.

Though Hands was wounded, he moved surprisingly fast. I saw no hope of escape.

Just then, though, the *Hispaniola*, balancing partly on water, partly on land, leaned sideways. The movement unfooted us both. We rolled down the deck, almost on top of each other.

I got on my feet first and climbed up the mast, high above Hands. With a moment to myself, I changed the priming on my pistol, making it ready to fire.

Hands saw the pistol. He put the knife in his teeth and began to climb up the mast after me. I aimed the pistol at him.

"One more step, Mr. Hands," said I, "and I'll shoot!"

"I reckon I'll have to strike," he said. To speak he had to take the knife from his mouth. He drew it far behind his shoulder. Then I heard something like an arrow singing through the air. I felt a blow, then a sharp pang. There I was, pinned to the mast, the knife sticking out of my shoulder.

In the surprise of the moment — I'm sure it was without aiming — both my pistols went off and fell from my hands. But they did not fall uselessly. With a choked cry, Hands let go of the mast and fell, head first, into the water.

I began to feel sick, faint, and terrified. The hot blood was running over my back and chest. I shuddered and that violent shaking freed me from the knife. It had held me by only a pinch of skin.

I climbed down the mast and went below deck to fix up my wound. When I came back up, I looked over the side of the boat. We were anchored in shallow water. I grabbed a rope and let myself drop overboard and waded ashore.

I was in great spirits. The *Hispaniola* was free of buccaneers at last. It was ready for our own men to board and sail to sea again. I thought of going back to the stockade and boasting of my adventures. Though I had deserted my side earlier, I believed that even the captain would be pleased with my achievements.

I set out for the log-house and my companions and soon came to the familiar clearing. There was a huge fire in the fireplace, bigger than the captain would have allowed. I began to fear that something had gone wrong.

I got on my hands and knees and crawled around the log-house. As I drew nearer, my heart lightened, for I heard a noise. It was a pleasant noise: my friends snoring together.

There was no doubt about one thing, though. They kept a bad watch. I blamed myself for leaving them with so few to keep guard.

I got the door open and stood up. The snoring continued. I walked in. I thought I would lie down in my own place and enjoy the look of their faces when they woke to see me in the morning.

My foot struck a leg, but even then the snoring continued. And then, all of a sudden, a shrill voice broke the silence.

"Ahoy, matey! Ahoy, matey!"

It was Silver's parrot, Cap'n Flint! I had no time to recover. Silver cried out: "Who goes?"

I turned to run but struck against one person then ran into the arms of another man. Someone lit a torch and I saw that the pirates had taken over the log-house!

I could only believe that all my friends had died. I wished at that moment that I had died along with them.

There were six pirates. Five of them were on their feet. The sixth was badly wounded.

"So here's Jim Hawkins, dropped in to see us," said Silver. "I take that as friendly. What a pleasant surprise. I see you were smart from the first time I set my eyes on you."

He believed that I had come over to their side.

"You can go back to your own lot," said Silver. "But I believe they won't have you. You'll have to join up with Captain Silver."

My friends, then, were alive. Though I was afraid that what Silver said about not taking me back was true.

"If I'm to choose," I said, growing bolder, "I believe I have a right to know what's what and where my friends are."

"Yesterday morning," said Silver, "Dr. Livesey came with a flag of truce. He said, 'All is gone. The ship's gone.' We looked out, and, by thunder, the ship was gone. It looked fishy. The doctor asked to strike a bargain. I bargained and here we are. We have the food, the log-house and the brandy. As for them, I don't know where they are.

"As for you, the doctor said, 'I don't know where the boy is and I don't much care. We're sick of him.' These were his words."

"And now am I to choose?" said I.

"And now you are to choose," said Silver.

"I've seen too many die since I fell in with you," I said. "You are in a bad way. The ship is lost. The treasure is lost. Men are lost. But the laugh's on my side. I heard you from the apple barrel that night, when you plotted to mutiny. And it was I who cut the ship loose. And I killed the men you left to watch her. I've been on top of this business from the first. But I'll say this. If you spare me now, when you fellows go to court for piracy, I'll save you all I can. I know the whole story. It is for you to choose."

I stopped, for I was out of breath. To my wonder, not a man moved. They stared at me like sheep.

Then one of the men said, "There he goes!" and pulled a cutlass, meaning to kill me.

"I'm captain here!" said Silver.

"And you'll obey me. I like that boy, now. I've never seen a better boy. He's more man than you rats."

Not a man stirred; not a man answered.

"Pardon, sir," said one of the men to Silver. "We don't like your bullying. We have a right to talk this over."

With that, the men stepped outside to discuss my fate while Silver stayed to talk to me.

"Now you look here, Jim Hawkins," he said, "you're within a half a plank of death. And what's worse, maybe torture. But I will stand by you and you will stand by me. I say, save your witness and he will save your neck!"

I began to understand that the pirates were in a bad way.

"You mean all's lost?" I asked.

"The ship's gone," he said. "When I saw that, I gave up. I'll save your life, best I can. But see here, Jim, you save Long John in court!"

"What I can do, I'll do," I said.

"It's a bargain!" cried Long John. "I've a chance."

Then he whispered to me. "I know you've got that ship safe somewheres. How you done it, I don't know. I know when a game's up, though. And I know a lad that's tough.

"What I don't know," he continued, "is why the doctor gave me the treasure chart. There's something at the bottom of that — good or bad."

The buccaneers returned to the log-house. One man, Dick, stepped forward and pressed something into Silver's hand.

"The black spot! I thought so," Silver said.

"Turn it over and see what's written there," said the pirate.

Silver turned it over. "'Deposed,' that's it! I'm deposed and you mean to make yourself captain. Well your black spot ain't worth a biscuit as long as I can speak the King's English! It was your bungling that very nearly sank the lot of us!"

Long John Silver looked at the men sternly.

"We're near to hanging for piracy," said Silver. "And my neck is sore to think of it. We have the boy as hostage. Are we going to waste a hostage? There will be a boat from England coming to save these gentlemen, you can be sure of that. And this boy as hostage can save us from hanging when they get here. But you came to bargain and I'll do that."

Silver threw a paper at their feet that I instantly recognized. It was the treasure chart. Why the doctor had given him the chart, I did not know. But the chart changed the mood of the mutineers.

They leapt upon it like cats on a mouse. It went from hand to hand and a childish laughter arose.

"But how are we to get the treasure away, with no ship?" said Dick.

"You lost the ship," said Silver. "But I found the treasure. Who's the better man? Now I can resign if you want me to."

"Silver!" they cried. "Silver for captain forever!"

"And now, the black spot," said Silver.

He tossed me the bit of paper for a souvenir.

I went to sleep that night, uneasy. Silver was holding the mutineers off with one hand, and keeping me safe to save himself with the other.

While I tossed and turned, Silver slept peacefully.

I awoke the next morning to a voice calling out to us from the woods.

"Log-house, ahoy!" it cried. "Here's the doctor!"

I was glad to hear the voice. But I remembered my desertion and I felt ashamed to look him in the face.

"Top of the morning to you, sir!" answered Silver.

The doctor came up to the log-house. He was here to treat the wounded pirates.

"We've quite a surprise for you," said Silver.

"Not Jim?" said the doctor.

It seemed seconds before the doctor was able to speak.

"Well, well," said the doctor. "Duty first. I will look at these patients of yours. Then I will have a word with Jim."

With one grim nod to me, he went to work among the sick.

The doctor gave some of the men medicine for malaria and then nodded his head in my direction.

"Now, I'll have a word with the boy," said the doctor.

"Hawkins, I have your word of honour not to skip away from me?" Silver asked.

I nodded in agreement and followed the doctor outside.

"The boy will tell you that I saved his life," said Silver to the doctor. Then he let us walk out of earshot.

"Well Jim," said the doctor. "You fled. That was cowardly."

I began to weep. "Doctor," I said, "I have blamed myself already. I would be dead now if Silver had not saved me. I can die. I daresay I deserve it, but I fear they will torture me."

"Jim," the doctor spoke in whisper, "I can't have this. Come here, and we'll make a run for it."

I shook my head. "I gave Silver my word."

"I'll take the shame for a broken word," said the doctor. "We'll make a run for it."

"I can't go back on my word," I said. "But doctor. If they come to torture me, I can tell them where the ship is. I got the ship! She lies in the North Inlet."

"The ship!" exclaimed the doctor.

I described my adventures to him. He heard me out in silence.

"Every step it is you who saves our lives," said the doctor. "Do you think we are going to let you lose yours?"

Then the doctor turned to Silver

who had come close.

"Silver," the doctor cried, "I give you a piece of advice. Don't be in too great a hurry to go after that treasure."

"I can only save my life and the boy's by seeking that treasure," said Silver. "Why you've given me that chart, I don't know. But if you tell me plain out why, I'll quit the search."

"No," said the doctor. "I have no right to say anything more. It's not my secret to share. But I'll tell you this, Silver. If we both get out alive, I'll do my best to save you, short of lying."

Silver's face lit up.

"But," the doctor continued, "keep this boy safe by you. When you need help, holler. Good-bye, Jim."

"Jim," said Silver when we were alone, "if I saved your life, you saved mine. I seen the doctor waving for you to make a run for it. I seen you say no. And now, Jim, we're going to go treasure-hunting. But you and me must stick close."

We returned to the mutineers in the log-house. They were eating breakfast.

"Sure enough, they have the ship," said Silver. "Where they have it, I don't know yet. But we will have the treasure."

Silver took out a length of rope and began to tie one end to me. He held the other in his hand so that I was tethered to him like a dog to his master.

"We'll keep this boy like gold," said Silver. "When we have the

treasure, we'll get the ship. We will all sail to sea like jolly companions!"

I set forth with my captors on the quest for treasure.

We stopped along the way to look at the chart. A red cross marked the place on the map where the treasure was buried.

A tall tree was to be our mark. We walked up to the highest point on Skeleton Island.

There, at the foot of a pretty pine, was a human skeleton. There were a few shreds of clothing on the ground.

"He was a seaman," said George Merry, who was bolder than the rest. "This is good sea-cloth."

When we got to the top of the hill, Silver took a bearing with his compass. "There are three tall trees," he said. "It's child's play to find the stuff now."

But the men were almost whispering now, still thinking of the skeleton. It was as if the dead Captain Flint had come to haunt us. Suddenly, we heard a cry:

> *"Fifteen men on the*
> *dead man's chest,*
> *Yo-yo-ho, and a*
> *bottle of rum!"*

The colour went out of the pirates' faces.

"It's Flint!" cried one.

"Come," said Silver. "Someone's tricking us."

Silver's own courage came back to him as he spoke.

Then the cry from the trees started up again: "Darby M'Graw! Fetch aft the rum, Darby!"

"They was the last words Flint spoke on the boat," moaned one pirate. "Nobody on this here island ever heard of Darby. Except us."

The pirates would have run away on the spot. But fear kept them close by Silver. He fought his own fear down.

"That voice doesn't sound like Flint's," he said. "No! It sounds like Ben Gunn's!"

"Well, dead or alive, nobody minds Ben Gunn!" said Merry George.

With that, their spirits returned, and we pushed on.

We reached the first of the tall trees. The third rose nearly 200 feet into the air. Its trunk was as big as a cottage. It could be seen

far out to sea from both the east and the west. And buried below it was gold.

I stumbled, trying to keep up to the pirates. The bushes around the tree were peaceful, but now they rang with pirates' cries for gold. Not 10 yards away was the tree. Then we came to a dead stop.

Before us was a huge hole. There was a broken pickax and boards from a packing case. On one of these boards was the name of Flint's ship: *The Walrus.*

We looked inside the hold. It was empty. The treasure had already been taken away!

The mutineers stopped as if they had been struck. But Silver was already thinking of his next plan. He handed me a pistol.

"Jim," he whispered. "Take that and stand by for trouble."

He began to inch away from the pirates. He looked at me with a friendly gaze. I could not help whispering, "So, you've changed sides again."

The buccaneers began to turn on Silver. There we stood, two against five, the empty pit between us.

Merry George raised his arm to lead a charge of the pirates against us. As he did, three musket shots flashed out of the woods. Merry tumbled into the pit and another man at his side fell dead. The other three turned and ran.

At that moment, the doctor, Gray, and Ben Gunn joined us.

"You came in the nick of time," Silver said, "for me and Hawkins."

But we did not have time to speak. We set off in chase of the pirates.

"We must head 'em off at the boats!" cried the doctor.

Silver, running on one leg with his crutch, could barely keep up. When we got to the edge of the hill, he was 30 yards behind us.

"Doctor!" he cried. "See there! No hurry!"

And there was not. We could see that the pirates were running toward the stockade. We were already between them and the boats.

We sat down to catch our breath. Silver greeted Ben Gunn and Ben told him his story.

It was Ben who had found the treasure. He had dug up the gold and carried it back to his cave. When the doctor heard this story from Ben, the doctor went to give the treasure map to Silver. Then the doctor and his companions moved into Ben's cave with the treasure.

The doctor began to fear for my life when he realized I would be with the pirates when they discovered the gold was missing. It was Ben Gunn's idea to try to scare them away. Failing that, they planned to ambush the pirates at the empty treasure pit.

"Ah, it was fortunate I had Jim Hawkins with me. Or you would have let old John be cut to bits," said Silver.

"And so we would have," said the doctor.

We walked back to the pirates' small boats. We destroyed one with a pickax and got in the other. We set sail for the North Inlet and the *Hispaniola*.

As we passed the two-pointed hill, we saw the mouth of Ben Gunn's cave. There, the squire and captain stood waving to us.

We boarded the *Hispaniola*. She was in good shape except for the wreck of her main sail. We left Gray to watch over the schooner, then set back for the cave. The squire met us.

"Silver," he said. "You're a villain and imposter. But I am told I am not to prosecute you. Well, then, I will not. But may the dead men, sir, hang about your neck like millstones."

"Thank you kindly, sir," said Long John Silver, saluting him.

We entered the cave. Before a big fire lay Captain Smollett and, in a far corner, great heaps of coin and bars of gold. That was Flint's treasure we had come so far to seek. And it had cost us the lives of 17 men.

"Come in, Jim," said the captain. "You're a good boy, but I don't think you and me'll go to sea again. And is that you, John Silver? What brings you here?"

"Come back to my booty, sir," returned Silver, eyeing the gold.

The next morning we went to work carrying the treasure to the ship. We heard nothing from the surviving mutineers for the three days we worked.

"They are drunk or raving mad," said Silver.

It was decided that we would desert them on the island. This delighted Ben Gunn.

We left them guns and powder, some goat meat, medicine and

some tools and clothes.

Then, one fine morning, we pulled up anchor. As we sailed away, we saw the three mutineers kneeling in the sand, crying out to us to take them.

It went to all our hearts, I think, to leave them. But we could not risk another mutiny.

We set course for the nearest port in Spanish America. We could not sail back to England without a fresh crew.

It was sundown when we sailed into the port of a beautiful island. We were immediately surrounded by shore boats. The natives of the island offered to sell us fresh fruits and vegetables. It was a charming place.

We met a captain of an English ship close by. The doctor and squire, taking me with them, went on board to talk. The others, except Ben Gunn and Silver, went to shore.

When we returned, Gunn made a confession. Silver was gone with one of the sacks of coin. Ben had helped him escape. He assured us that it was to save all of our lives.

I think we were all pleased that the one-legged sea cook was gone.

To make a long story short, we got fresh hands, sailed back to Bristol, just as a search boat was getting ready to come after us.

Only five who started the voyage returned. All of us had a good share of the treasure. Captain Smollett retired on his share; Gray saved his money, studied his profession and became part-owner of a ship; Ben Gunn got a thousand pounds, which he spent in 19 days and went begging on the 20th.

We heard no more of Silver. Perhaps he met up with Captain Flint or is living in comfort somewhere. That is well, for his chances of comfort in another world are very small.

There are still bars of silver on the island where Flint buried them under another red cross. But nothing would ever draw me back to Treasure Island. The worst dreams I have are of the island and the sharp voice of the parrot, Cap'n Flint, crying, "Ahoy, matey! Ahoy, matey!"